Feelings

Impatient

Sarah Medina

Illustrated by Jo Brooker

www.raintreepublishers.co.uk
Visit our website to find out more information about **Raintree** books.

To order:
☎ Phone 44 (0) 1865 888112
▤ Send a fax to 44 (0) 1865 314091
▦ Visit the Raintree Bookshop at **www.raintreepublishers.co.uk** to browse our catalogue and order online.

First published in Great Britain by Raintree,
Halley Court, Jordan Hill, Oxford OX2 8EJ,
part of Harcourt Education.
Raintree is a registered trademark of
Harcourt Education Ltd.

Editorial: Diyan Leake and Cassie Mayer
Design: Joanna Hinton-Malivoire
Picture research: Erica Martin
Illustration: Jo Brooker
Production: Duncan Gilbert

Originated by Modern Age
Printed and bound in China by
  South China Printing Company

ISBN 978 1 4062 0781 1

12 11 10 09 08
10 9 8 7 6 5 4 3 2 1

British Library Cataloguing in Publication Data
Medina, Sarah
  Impatient. - (Feelings)
  1. Patience - Juvenile literature
  I. Title
  152.2'32

Acknowledgements
The publishers would like to thank the following
for permission to reproduce photographs:
Bananastock p. **22 A, B, D**; Getty Images/Taxi
p. **22C**.

Every effort has been made to contact copyright
holders of any material reproduced in this book.
Any omissions will be rectified in subsequent
printings if notice is given to the publishers.

Contents

Some words are shown in bold, **like this**. They are explained in the glossary on page 23.

What is impatience?

Impatience is a **feeling**. Feelings are something you feel inside. Everyone has different feelings all the time.

jealous

caring

sad

4

When you feel impatient, you want
something to happen right now. You
do not want to wait.

5

What happens when I am impatient?

Impatience can make you want to whine or shout. You may burst into tears.

If you are impatient, you may want to grab something that someone else has got.

Why do I feel impatient?

You might feel impatient if you have to do something you do not want to do, like going on a long journey.

You might feel impatient if you find
something hard to learn or finish.

Is it OK to feel impatient?

It is normal to feel impatient sometimes. The important thing is what you do when you feel impatient.

When you feel impatient, you should never **upset** anyone with what you say or do.

What can I do if I feel impatient?

1, 2, 3, 4 ...

If you feel impatient, count to ten before you do or say anything. This might help you **calm** down.

If you can, tell someone that you feel impatient. Or try doing something fun that you enjoy!

Will I always feel impatient?

Feelings change all the time.
Impatience does not last long. You
will soon feel better.

Practise ways to stop feeling impatient.

How can I tell if someone is impatient?

When people feel impatient, they may look angry. They might talk loudly or shout at you.

They may be bossy and tell you what to do. They may not listen to you.

Can I help when someone is impatient?

When people are impatient, try not to get impatient, too. Stay **calm** and say quietly that they should play nicely.

If they are finding something hard, offer to help them. Do not worry if they do not want your help.

Am I the only one who feels impatient?

Remember, everyone feels impatient sometimes.

It is good to learn what to do when you feel impatient. Being happy is much more fun!

What are these feelings?

A

B

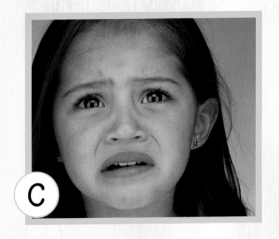

C

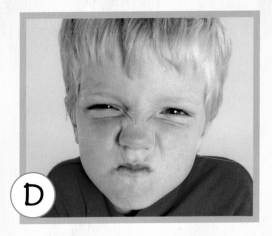

D

Which of these people looks happy?
What are the other people feeling?

Look at page 24 to see the answer.

Picture glossary

calm
quiet inside

feeling
something that you feel
inside. Impatience is
a feeling.

upset
make someone sad, or even
make them cry

Index

Answers to the questions on page 22
The person in picture B looks happy. The other people could be impatient, angry, or sad.

Note to Parents and Teachers
Reading for information is an important part of a child's literacy development. Learning begins with a question about something. Help children think of themselves as investigators and researchers by encouraging their questions about the world around them. Most chapters in this book begin with a question. Read the question together. Look at the pictures. Talk about what you think the answer might be. Then read the text to find out if your predictions were correct. Think of other questions you could ask about the topic, and discuss where you might find the answers. Assist children in using the picture glossary and the index to practice new vocabulary and research skills.